Hillside Lullaby

by **Hope Vestergaard**  illustrated by **Margie Moore**

Dutton Children's Books

DUTTON CHILDREN'S BOOKS
A division of Penguin Young Readers Group

Published by the Penguin Group

Penguin Group (USA) Inc., 375 Hudson Street, New York, New York 10014, U.S.A.
Penguin Group (Canada), 90 Eglinton Avenue East, Suite 700, Toronto, Ontario, Canada M4P 2Y3 (a division of Pearson Penguin Canada Inc.)
Penguin Books Ltd, 80 Strand, London WC2R 0RL, England
Penguin Ireland, 25 St Stephen's Green, Dublin 2, Ireland (a division of Penguin Books Ltd)
Penguin Group (Australia), 250 Camberwell Road, Camberwell, Victoria 3124, Australia (a division of Pearson Australia Group Pty Ltd)
Penguin Books India Pvt Ltd, 11 Community Centre, Panchsheel Park, New Delhi - 110 017, India
Penguin Group (NZ), Cnr Airborne and Rosedale Roads, Albany, Auckland 1310, New Zealand (a division of Pearson New Zealand Ltd)
Penguin Books (South Africa) (Pty) Ltd, 24 Sturdee Avenue, Rosebank, Johannesburg 2196, South Africa
Penguin Books Ltd, Registered Offices: 80 Strand, London WC2R 0RL, England

Text copyright © 2006 by Hope Vestergaard

Illustrations copyright © 2006 by Margie Moore

LIBRARY OF CONGRESS CATALOGING-IN-PUBLICATION DATA

Vestergaard, Hope.
Hillside lullaby / by Hope Vestergaard; illustrations by Margie Moore.— 1st ed.
p. cm.
Summary: A wild child is not ready for bed, but all around her are animals settling in for the night to the tune of a hillside song.
ISBN 0-525-47215-0
[1. Bedtime—Fiction. 2. Animals—Fiction. 3. Stories in rhyme.] I. Moore, Margie, ill.
II. Title.
PZ8.3.V57Hi 2006
[E]—dc21   2003045220

Published in the United States by Dutton Children's Books,
a division of Penguin Young Readers Group
345 Hudson Street, New York, New York 10014
www.penguin.com/youngreaders

Designed by Beth Herzog and Gloria Cheng

Manufactured in China   First Edition

1 3 5 7 9 10 8 6 4 2

For Reese—one wild little child
H.V.

For my father
M.M.

In a house on a hill
there's a wild little child
not ready to close her eyes.

She burrows in blankets
and talks to her toys
and listens for lullabies.

Twilight.
   Sleep tight!

There's a chick in the thicket
who's thirsty for dew,
which he chirps for his mom to bring.

She flies off to fetch it

and fills up his beak,
then tucks him beneath her wing.

Coo, coo.
Love you!

There are hares in the garden
who won't hop off to bed.
So their mom gives them one last chase.

They end in their den,
cuddled close, tails to toes—
it's a crowded but cozy place.

Sweet clover.
Scoot over!

There's a breeze on the hill
blowing sleepy and fresh,
like the breath of the harvest moon.
And tucked in the cattails,
a bold little toad
echoes his mother's tune.

Peep, peep.

Dream deep!

There's a log on the hill
where raccoons stop to snack
after washing their paws and cheeks.
Their mom licks their whiskers
and fluffs up their tails
and shushes their playful squeaks.

Tall trees.
Quiet, please!

There's a fawn in the meadow
who's frolicked all day.
She's munching a bedtime snack.
Her mom walks in circles
to tramp down a bed,

then nuzzles her baby's back.

No fear.
'Night, dear.

There's a cricket in tall grass.
He's tuning his wings
and learning the hillside song.
His mom plays beside him,
a chorus of strings.
The whole hillside sings along.

In her house on the hillside,
one tired little child
snuggles down in her big, soft bed.

She's dreaming sweet dreams . . .
and hearing sweet sounds . . .
with the song of the hill in her head.

Starlight.
Good night!